Dear Parents:

Congratulations! Your child . the first steps on an exciting journey. The destination? Independent reading!

STEP INTO READING® will help your child get there. The program offers five steps to reading success. Each step includes fun stories and colorful art or photographs. In addition to original fiction and books with favorite characters, there are Step into Reading Non-Fiction Readers, Phonics Readers and Boxed Sets, Sticker Readers, and Comic Readers—a complete literacy program with something to interest every child.

Learning to Read, Step by Step!

Ready to Read   Preschool–Kindergarten
• big type and easy words • rhyme and rhythm • picture clues
For children who know the alphabet and are eager to begin reading.

Reading with Help   Preschool–Grade 1
• basic vocabulary • short sentences • simple stories
For children who recognize familiar words and sound out new words with help.

Reading on Your Own   Grades 1–3
• engaging characters • easy-to-follow plots • popular topics
For children who are ready to read on their own.

Reading Paragraphs   Grades 2–3
• challenging vocabulary • short paragraphs • exciting stories
For newly independent readers who read simple sentences with confidence.

Ready for Chapters   Grades 2–4
• chapters • longer paragraphs • full-color art
For children who want to take the plunge into chapter books but still like colorful pictures.

STEP INTO READING® is designed to give every child a successful reading experience. The grade levels are only guides; children will progress through the steps at their own speed, developing confidence in their reading.

Remember, a lifetime love of reading starts with a single step!

Manufactured under license granted to AMEET Sp. z o.o. by the LEGO Group.

AMEET Sp. z o.o.
Nowe Sady 6, 94-102 Łódź—Poland
ameet@ameet.eu
www.ameet.eu

www.LEGO.com

Published in the United States by Random House Children's Books, a division of Penguin Random House LLC, 1745 Broadway, New York, NY 10019, and in Canada by Penguin Random House Canada Limited, Toronto.

Step into Reading, Random House, and the Random House colophon are registered trademarks of Penguin Random House LLC.

Visit us on the Web!
rhcbooks.com

Educators and librarians, for a variety of teaching tools, visit us at RHTeachersLibrarians.com

ISBN 978-0-593-80894-8 (trade)
ISBN 978-0-593-80895-5 (lib. bdg.)
ISBN 978-0-593-80896-2 (ebook)

MANUFACTURED IN CHINA

10 9 8 7 6 5 4 3 2 1

GAME ON!

by Steve Foxe

based on the story by Meredith Rusu

illustrated by AMEET Studio

Random House 🏠 New York

The lights flashed, the crowd cheered, and the Stunt Team got ready for their final trick. Rocket Racer, Wallop, Spotlight, Raze, and Viper were about to pull off a midair bike swap.

"You're in for a wicked surprise!"
Viper said, grinning. She lowered
her helmet face shield.
"I've put something at the end
to make our stunt extra fun!"

The Stunt Team sped up
the motorcycle ramp.
Vroom!
The riders were going to
swap vehicles in midair!
It was the perfect team trick!

But while the racers were

soaring through the air,

they looked down to see

a giant pit of snakes below them!

"AHHHH!" everyone except

Viper screamed as they fell in.

Rocket Racer was confused after
they'd landed in the squishy pit.
"These snakes are just foam!"
Viper started laughing.

"Of course they are,"
she replied. "I wanted to
make our stunt fun, not fangy!"
The crowd loved it.
They went wild with applause!

While the team signed autographs,

a woman came over.

"I work at Game On Game Designs,"

she said. "And I want one

of you to be the hero of

my new stunt-racing game!"

Rocket Racer shook his head.
"Sorry, but we do our best
tricks as a team."
Then, to Rocket's surprise,
his friends were suddenly eager
to show off their solo tricks.

"Our odds of success are
much higher when we work
as a team," Rocket Racer insisted.
But the video game designer
was watching. It was go time!

Wallop was up first.

"I'm going to zigzag through wrecking balls," he explained. "I call this Dash or Get Bashed!" Rocket Racer was worried. He didn't think Dash could dodge ALL the wrecking balls.

But Wallop wasn't listening.

Wallop zigged left.

He zagged right.

Until . . . *BASH!*

The final wrecking ball

sent him flying through the sky!

FWOOP!

Wallop landed safely on top of
a blimp that was floating over the city.
"Now *that's* what I call a bash!"
he exclaimed.

After Wallop was rescued,

it was Spotlight's turn.

"For my trick, I'm going to ride

backward, standing up,

while live-streaming!"

The tape attaching Spotlight's

phone to his bike

was already peeling off.

Rocket Racer said he'd

film Spotlight, but

Spotlight insisted that

he could do it himself.

As Spotlight sped off,

his phone rang. It was

his grandmother calling!

"Grandma!" Spotlight cried.

"I can't talk now!"

But the vibration of the phone

ringing had knocked it loose.

Spotlight toppled off his bike.
The bike zoomed on
and just missed crushing
his phone by a few inches!

"I'm up next!" Viper said.
A crew wheeled out
a massive obstacle that looked
like a giant python.
"I'm going to sail into its mouth
and do a wheelie down its back!"

In a blur, Viper rocketed off the bike ramp, pointed straight between the python's fangs. She was going to make it!

Then, suddenly . . .

Snag!

One of Viper's

helmet tassels

got caught

on a top fang!

"We have to help!" Raze shouted.

"Quick, move the snake pit,"

said Rocket Racer.

Working together, the team

positioned it under Viper.

Viper fell safely into the pit.

"Thanks, guys! Saved by snakes!

Who'da thought?"

Then it was Raze's turn.

"For my trick, I'm using math
to run the course in record time."

Rocket Racer was excited.

He offered to check her math,

but Raze was very confident.

She whizzed around the spiral.

She swooped up the loop-de-loop.

She sailed across the finish line!
But the game designer checked
her stopwatch. Raze was
one second short of the record!

ALMOST
NEW RECORD
09:53

"You'll break that record
next time for sure,"
Rocket said to Raze.
Raze asked Rocket,
"What's your trick going to be?"
Rocket shook his head.
"I already told you, I perform
my best when we work together."

As the team rode off,

the game designer smiled and

wrote down a few final notes. . . .

A few weeks later, the big
video game reveal day arrived.
"Which one of us do you
think she chose as the hero?"
Spotlight asked.
But no one on the Stunt Team
was prepared for the answer.

She had decided that the game
had *five* main heroes!
"Your teamwork inspired me,"
the game designer explained.
"I couldn't choose just one of you!"

The Stunt Team grinned proudly.

Rocket Racer high-fived

each of them.

"Like I said, our odds of success

are always at their highest

when we work as a team!"